The Dragon Who Wanted to Fly

The Dragon Who Wanted to Fly

by Jeffrey Comanor

Turner Publishing, Inc.

ATLANTA

GRANDMA'S NOTE TO THE PUBLISHER

Dear Sir or Madam,

Down in a dark corner of his old Uncle Godfrey's cellar...

my grandson Jeffrey found an ancient trunk.

Inside were all kinds of interesting & peculiar items...

for instance...

 silver buttons,

a stuffed
ballaboo,

and some homemade books
filled with drawings and
 tied together
with ribbons.

Here is one of them.

Yours truly,
Grandma Comanor

Once, in the Far Country, there lived a dragon. His name was Fedge, and he was very unhappy. You see, he had not always lived in the Far Country.

He used to live on the warm, happy Island of Dandy with his friends Snord and Huff. Then, one black day, he was carried off by the hairy condor Snooch (a local troublemaker)

and deposited
in the
Far Country,
homeless.

It happened that one
bleak morning Fedge
decided to figure out a
way to go home again.

He thought...

 and he thought...

and suddenly,
he had an
IDEA.

Why,

he would

fly,

of course!

Now, you 😊 know

and I 🧑 know

that dragons

have

no

wings!

(just a lot of scales)

But one thing about dragons— once they have made up their minds, they are pretty determined.

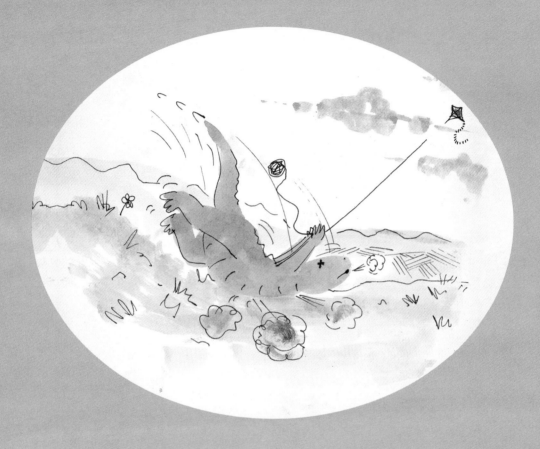

And even if at
first they do not
succeed...

they try,

try
again.

Nothing
seemed
to work.

(Poor Fedge!)

The days
dragged on, and so
did Fedge.

Winter came...
and went.

And spring came...
and went.

And summer came.

One particularly

hot day,

Fedge went for

a walk

in the park.

As he stepped
around a corner,

his eyes
bugged out,

and he gave a great

cry of joy!

For there,
just ahead,
was the answer
to the
problem!

(Guess.)

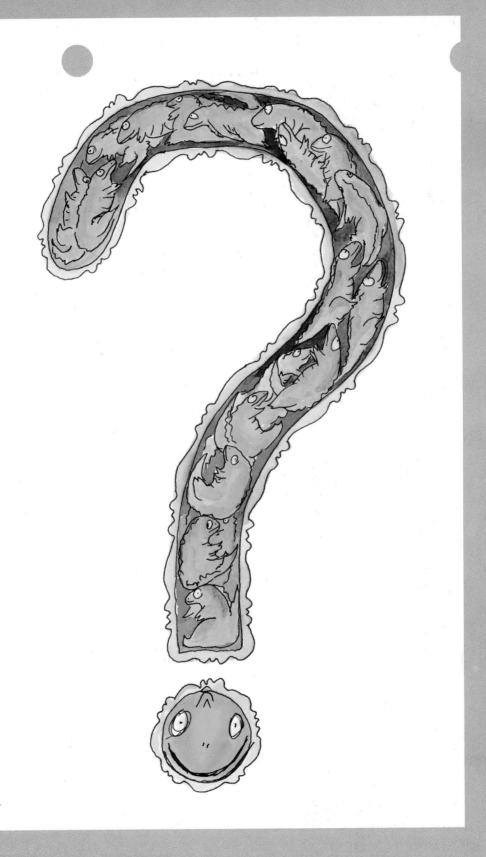

I bet you know what is going to happen now.

Got it?

You are right!

Fedge took
hold of
the balloons,
and
up he went.

Unfortunately, Fedge found out that just going up does not mean going home.

There was no wind to push Fedge along, so he just floated in one place.

The sun began to get hotter. Soon Fedge was uncomfortably warm.

He started to fan himself.

Then something wonderful happened!

He
started
to move!

The faster he fanned, the faster he went.

Fedge began the long trip home.

Soon...

Fedge
was
home
again!

His friends were

overjoyed to

see him.

Snord

snorted, and

Huff

huffed.

Together
they gave
him a
beautiful
welcome home
party.

And they lived very happily together for a long, long, long, time.

...and by the way, this book's for Faye

PUBLISHED BY TURNER PUBLISHING, INC.
A SUBSIDIARY OF TURNER BROADCASTING SYSTEM, INC.
1050 TECHWOOD DRIVE, N.W.
ATLANTA, GEORGIA 30318

Library of Congress Cataloging-in-Publication Data
Comanor, Jeffrey.
The dragon who wanted to fly/by Jeffrey Comanor.–1st ed.
          p.   cm.
Summary: Having been snatched up by a hairy condor and dropped in the Far Country,
Fedge the dragon keeps on trying to fly so that he can return home.
ISBN 1-57036-202-5
[1. Dragons–Fiction. 2. Flight–Fiction. 3. Perseverance (Ethics)–Fiction. 4. Home–Fiction.]
I. Title.
PZ7.C7295Dr   1995
[E]–DC20   94-40726
                                                           CIP
                                                           AC

DISTRIBUTED BY ANDREWS AND MCMEEL
A UNIVERSAL PRESS SYNDICATE COMPANY
4900 MAIN STREET
KANSAS CITY, MISSOURI 64112

FIRST EDITION 10 9 8 7 6 5 4 3 2 1

DESIGNER: MICHAEL J. WALSH
EDITOR: ALAN AXELROD

MANUFACTURED IN CHINA